Note to parents, carers and teachers

Read it yourself is a series of modern stories, favourite characters and traditional tales written in a simple way for children who are learning to read. The books can be read independently or as part of a guided reading session.

Each book is carefully structured to include many high-frequency words vital for first reading. The sentences on each page are supported closely by pictures to help with understanding, and to offer lively details to talk about.

The books are graded into four levels that progressively introduce wider vocabulary and longer stories as a reader's ability and confidence grows.

Ideas for use

- Although your child will now be progressing towards silent, independent reading, let her know that your help and encouragement is always available.

- Developing readers can be concentrating so hard on the words that they sometimes don't fully grasp the meaning of what they're reading. Answering the puzzle questions at the end of the book will help with understanding.

For more information and advice on Read it yourself and book banding, visit **www.ladybird.com/readityourself**

Book Band 9

Level 4 is ideal for children who are ready to read longer stories with a wider vocabulary and are eager to start reading independently.

Special features:

Clear type

Full, exciting story

Richer, more varied vocabulary

Po and Tigress grabbed the statue. The Crocs came after them.

"You take half, and I'll take half!" said Po.

But there were so many Crocs to fight!

"We need a plan!" cried Po. "We need to do this together!"

Longer sentences

Detailed illustrations capture the imagination

The fight was going their way, until . . .

"Ha-ha!" cried Fung.

He had grabbed the statue and the ruby – and he was getting away!

Po and Tigress had to stop him!

Educational Consultant: Geraldine Taylor
Book Banding Consultant: Kate Ruttle

LADYBIRD BOOKS

UK | USA | Canada | Ireland | Australia
India | New Zealand | South Africa

Ladybird Books is part of the Penguin Random House group of companies
whose addresses can be found at global.penguinrandomhouse.com.

www.penguin.co.uk   www.puffin.co.uk   www.ladybird.co.uk

First published 2016
This edition published 2017
001

Printed in China

A CIP catalogue record for this book is available from the British Library

ISBN: 978-0-241-24981-9

All correspondence to:
Ladybird Books
Penguin Random House Children's
80 Strand, London WC2R 0RL

Friends Stick Together

Adaptation written by
Richard Dungworth

Po and Tigress were on a mission.

Shifu had sent them to bring home his best statue – the one with the ruby.

Po did not stop talking all the way there.

"Po!" said Tigress. "Don't talk all the time! We're on a mission!"

Suddenly, the statue slipped.

Po and Tigress grabbed at it, and . . .

. . . CLANK!

– someone chained their
wrists together!

It was mean old Fung and his Crocs!

They attacked Po and Tigress.

"Get the ruby!" cried Fung.

Po and Tigress tried to fight back

"SHAK-A BOO-OOOF!"

But they got tangled up in the chain!

The Crocs backed Po and Tigress
up to a cliff.

"We can take them!" said Tigress.

Po looked at all the Crocs.
He looked at Tigress.

"Don't be mad at me," said Po.

And he jumped off the cliff!

Down, down, down went
Po and Tigress, before –

"OOOF!"

Their chain got tangled on a tree!

It had saved them from getting hurt!

"Ha-ha!" cried Po. "And I still have the ruby!"

"But we lost Shifu's best statue!" said Tigress.

"We can get the statue back," said Po.

"Not until we get this chain off!" said Tigress.

Before they had time to think how, the Crocs came after them.

Tigress took off into the forest, pulling Po behind her.

old temple.

The Crocs were not far behind. They tried to smash their way through the temple wall.

"We need to find another way out of here!" said Tigress.

Tigress grabbed the chain.
She swung it round and round
so that Po went flying round
and round, too!

CRASH!

Po hit the temple wall and smashed right through. Then he and Tigress went into the forest.

They had lost Fung and the Crocs!

Tigress worked on making a
fire and making a plan!

"I can make a key for the chain
from a stick," she thought.

"Po!" cried Tigress.
"That was my key!"

She was not pleased!

"Why don't you think, Po?"

"You don't think Oogway should have made me the Dragon Warrior, do you, Tigress?" said Po.

Tigress was still mad, so she just looked away.

Po was hurt.

"I'm out of here!" he said.

Po did not get far.

He licked some honey from his wrist and suddenly it hit him.

He was free! The honey had made the chain slip off!

Po ran back to find Tigress . . .

But Tigress was not there!

He went after them. He had
to find Tigress!

Po ran into the camp to free Tigress.

He smashed the post in half with
a flying kick.

"SHAK-A-BOOM!"

CRASH!

"Time to get that statue back!"
he said.

Po and Tigress grabbed the statue.
The Crocs came after them.

"You take half, and I'll take half!"
said Po.

But there were so many Crocs to fight!

"We need a plan!" cried Po. "We need
to do this together!"

Suddenly – CLANK!

Tigress put the chain back round Po's wrist!

"Tigress!" cried Po. "Why did you do that?"

"Because you're right!" said Tigress, smiling at him.

Then Po smiled, too.

"Together!" cried Po and Tigress.

They pulled on the chain and took out three Crocs at a time!

Then Tigress swung Po round and round.

Po attacked another three Crocs – the flying-Po way!

The fight was going their
way, until . . .

"Ha-ha!" cried Fung.

He had grabbed the statue and the
ruby – and he was getting away!

Po and Tigress had to stop him!

Together, Po and Tigress used the chain to bring Fung down.

Together, they tied him up with it.

And together, with the chain, they sent Fung flying far, far away.

They had saved Shifu's ruby statue!

"Good work, Po!" said Tigress. "Oogway was right. You're the one. You should be the Dragon Warrior."

"You mean it?" said Po. And he was so pleased . . . that he did not stop talking, all the way home!

How much do you remember about the story of Kung Fu Panda: Friends Stick Together? Answer these questions and find out!

- What mission are Po and Tigress on?

- Who is the leader of the Crocs?

- How do Po and Tigress escape from the temple?

- What does Tigress try to make from a stick?

- How does the chain come off Po's wrist?

- How does Po set Tigress free from the Crocs?

Unjumble these words to make words
from the story, then match them to the
correct pictures.

Trigses   tauset   ybur

hican   Csrco   yenho

Tick the books you've read!

Level 1

 Goldilocks and the Three Bears ☐
 The Magic Porridge Pot ☐
 The Tale of Peter Rabbit ☐
 The Ugly Duckling ☐
 Going Boating ☐

 Topsy + Tim At the Farm ☐
 Going Swimming ☐
 I am a Doctor ☐
 The Bravest Fox ☐
 The Big Pancake ☐

Level 2

 The Gingerbread Man ☐
 Little Red Riding Hood ☐
 Playing Football ☐
 Daddy Pig's Office ☐
 Sleeping Beauty ☐

 The Great Dragon Party ☐
 The Three Little Pigs ☐
 Superhero Max ☐
 The Monster Next Door ☐
 Jemima Puddle-Duck ☐

Level 3

 Harry and the Bucketful of Dinosaurs ☐
 Jack and the Beanstalk ☐
 The Jungle Book ☐
 Puss in Boots ☐
 The Elves and the Shoemaker ☐

Level 4

 I am Inventing an INVENTION ☐
 Kung Fu Panda FRIENDS STICK TOGETHER ☐
 The Little Mermaid ☐
 The Wizard of Oz ☐
 Snow White and the Seven Dwarfs ☐